ZAPATO POWER

FREDDIE RAMOS AND THE METEORITE

JACQUELINE JULES   art by KEIRON WARD

albert Whitman & Company
Chicago, Illinois

Don't miss the other **Zapato Power** books!

Freddie Ramos Takes Off
Freddie Ramos Springs into Action
Freddie Ramos Zooms to the Rescue
Freddie Ramos Makes a Splash
Freddie Ramos Stomps the Snow
Freddie Ramos Rules New York
Freddie Ramos Hears It All
Freddie Ramos Adds It All Up
Freddie Ramos Tracks Down a Drone
Freddie Ramos Gets a Sidekick

Library of Congress Cataloging-in-Publication
data is on file with the publisher.
Text copyright © 2021 by Jacqueline Jules
Illustrations copyright © 2021 by Albert Whitman & Company
Illustrations by Keiron Ward
First published in the United States of America
in 2021 by Albert Whitman & Company
ISBN 978-0-8075-9570-1 (hardcover)
ISBN 978-0-8075-9571-8 (ebook)

Printed in the United States of America

10 9 8 7 6 5 4 3 2 1 LB 24 23 22 21 20

Design by Valerie Hernández

For more information about Albert Whitman & Company,
visit our website at www.albertwhitman.com.

Contents

1. A Rock from Outer Space

On Sunday night, Mr. Vaslov
came to dinner. He takes care of
Starwood Park, where I live, and
he's my friend. He's also friends
with my mom and her boyfriend,
David. Mr. Vaslov and David both
like scientific stuff, especially
drones. They did a lot of talking

over a roasted chicken.

I don't mind sitting around a table with grown-ups, as long as I get ice cream for dessert. But that night, I needed to talk to Mr. Vaslov in private. So I asked Mom if I could walk Mr. Vaslov home. My plan didn't quite work.

"*Buena idea*," Mom said. "It's a pretty night. Let's all go."

Outside my apartment, 29G, Mr. Vaslov got on his red electric scooter—the one he uses to get around Starwood Park because he has bad knees. Mom and David walked on one side of Mr. Vaslov

while I walked on the other. No
one said much until we saw a ball
of fire streak through the night sky.
   "Look!" Mr. Vaslov shouted.
   We stayed still, our eyes up,
watching the bright light speed

down toward Earth. The light disappeared just beyond Starwood Park, near my school, Starwood Elementary.

"Wow!" David whistled.

"A meteor!" Mr. Vaslov clapped like a little kid getting candy.

"What's a meteor?" I asked.

"Good question, Freddie," Mr. Vaslov said. "A meteor is a rock falling to Earth from outer space."

"Did it land near here?" I asked.

"If it did," Mr. Vaslov said, "we might be able to find a meteorite. That's what you call a piece of space debris which reaches Earth."

"That would be amazing!" David said.

"A scientist's dream," Mr. Vaslov agreed.

Right away, I wanted to give Mr. Vaslov his dream. He'd made a dream come true for me. Because of Mr. Vaslov, I have Zapato Power. I can run ninety miles an hour, jump super high, and hear from far away.

My superpowers come from special purple sneakers Mr. Vaslov invented. The things he creates are even more amazing than a rock from outer space.

"I'm going to find your

meteorite," I told him. "I promise."

The very next morning, I started
looking before school.

ZOOM! ZOOM! ZAPATO!

I collected every rock I could
find and dropped them outside Mr.
Vaslov's toolshed, the place where
he works on his special inventions.

There were a lot more rocks
around Starwood Park than I ever
realized. It wasn't long before I
had a big pile. Which one was the
meteorite? Was it the smooth, sandy-
colored one or the spotted pebble? I
couldn't wait to show Mr. Vaslov.

Someone else met me at the toolshed first.

"Why are you collecting rocks, Freddie?" a girl's voice asked.

Amy! Every time I turned around, she was there. And she was always asking the same question.

"Can I help?"

Amy had Zapato Power shoes too. She was a first grader. Mr. Vaslov gave her the pair of sneakers I outgrew. He said we should be a team. That's what I had wanted to talk to Mr. Vaslov about in private. Amy was running to be a hero every chance she got, taking jobs away from me.

"What do we have here?" Mr. Vaslov rode up on his electric scooter.

"Lots of rocks," Amy said.

Mr. Vaslov smiled. "So you're trying to find the meteorite."

"Of course," I said. "You want it."

"I do," Mr. Vaslov said. "But these aren't meteorites."

"How do you know?" Amy asked.

"A fresh meteorite is black," Mr. Vaslov said. "The rock burns as it enters Earth's atmosphere. A meteorite also has an odd, irregular shape."

"I'm on it," Amy said. "A black rock that's not round."

She touched her silver wristband, which controlled her super speed.

ZIP! ZIP! ZAPATO

Amy was off, and I was right

behind her. This was my superhero job, and no one was going to steal it from me.

2. The Old Garden

I ran toward Starwood Elementary
since I hadn't looked there yet,
and it was almost time for school
to start.

ZOOM! ZOOM! ZAPATO!

I circled the playground twice.
No sign of black rocks. So I zoomed

past the front doors and around the corner to the far side of the building, where there used to be a school garden. Now it was a place with a lot of weeds.

SPLAT!

OUCH! I should have looked where I was going. The old garden had wooden boxes for planting, hidden underneath the weeds.

"Freddie!" Amy called. "Did you trip?"

Why was Amy *always* around?

ZIP! ZIP! ZAPATO

She rushed to my side and
helped me up.

"Are you hurt?" she asked.

I checked myself over. "I'm
dirty, not hurt."

"Great!" Amy said. "Let's look
for black rocks together."

We poked through the weeds
in the old garden while Amy

asked questions.

"Why is this place a mess? What used to be here?"

I told Amy what I knew. Starwood Elementary had a garden the year I moved to Starwood Park. Every grade had its own big wooden box for growing vegetables.

"Did you like it?" Amy asked.

"Everybody did," I said. "It was fun to grow stuff."

"How come no one takes care of the garden now?" Amy asked.

I shrugged. "Ask a teacher."

RING! RING!

The tardy bell! I needed to get moving before Mrs. Connor, the principal, caught me in the hallway again.

ZOOM! ZOOM! zapaTo!

ZIP! ZIP! zapaTo

Amy was right beside me when I sailed through the front door. We saw Mrs. Connor coming out of the main office.

"Freddie! Amy! What are you doing in the hallway?"

This was not the first time Mrs. Connor had asked me that question. I was running out of excuses.

Amy stepped in with the truth. Mostly.

"Freddie fell down in the grass," she said. "I helped him up."

Mrs. Connor looked at my knees and saw the evidence.

Green smudges on my jeans.

"All right." She waved her hand. "Go on."

As we walked to our classrooms, Amy asked me to meet her after school.

I couldn't say no. She'd just saved me from the principal.

At the end of the day, we met at the back door.

"I'm ready!" Amy said. "Let's go look for rocks!"

ZIP! ZIP! ZAPATO

ZOOM! ZOOM! ZAPATO!

We searched up and down Starwood Park. There were lots of sandy-colored and gray rocks. It took us a long time to find some black ones.

When we brought them to

Mr. Vaslov's toolshed, he came out with a horseshoe magnet.

"Most meteorites contain iron," Mr. Vaslov explained, "so they will stick to a magnet."

We held our breath while Mr. Vaslov tested our rocks. They didn't stick. Mr. Vaslov looked disappointed.

"Finding a meteorite isn't easy," he said.

"We'll keep looking," I told him.

"We won't give up," Amy promised, taking off.

ZIP! ZIP! ZAPATO

I was right behind her.

ZOOM! ZOOM! ZAPATO!

This time we didn't find any black rocks at all.

Amy was worried. "Super speed isn't helping."

She was right. We needed an extra power for this job. I rubbed the buttons on my purple wristband to turn on my super hearing.

"Meteorites are from space," she

said. "Maybe they beep."

"That's just what I was thinking!"

Amy's Zapato Power shoes gave her super speed, but not super hearing or super bounce, like mine.

"Do you hear anything?" she asked.

I shook my head. No clicking, fizzing, or beeping. Nothing that sounded like it came from outer space.

But I did hear voices. Mrs. Connor and Amy's teacher, Mr. Newton, were talking beside the old garden. They said Amy's name. And something I knew would make her very happy.

"What are they saying, Freddie?" she asked. "Why are they pointing at the garden?"

3. Plant Crazy

Super hearing is not for snooping. But since I'd already heard what Mrs. Connor and Mr. Newton said, I figured it was all right to tell Amy.

"Mr. Newton told Mrs. Connor that you asked about the garden. He said you reminded him how much everybody learned about plants."

"Really?" Amy clapped.

I nodded. "Mrs. Connor agreed that it's a good time to start the garden again."

"Wow!" Amy grinned. "I made a difference."

"But you can't tell anybody," I warned her. "I try to use my super hearing for helping people, not for finding out stuff grown-ups haven't told me yet."

"I'll keep it secret," Amy promised.

ZIP! ZIP! ZAPaTO

ZOOM! ZOOM! ZaPaTO!

We headed home, with Amy leading the way.

If we'd been running a race to Starwood Park, Amy would have won. She was always a few steps ahead. Were her Zapato Power shoes faster than mine? The thought bothered me all the way to 29G.

But as soon as I stepped inside my apartment, my guinea pig, Claude the Second, cheered me up.

WHEET! WHEET!

Claude the Second thinks

making noise will get him a carrot treat. He's right.

CHOMP! CHOMP!

While he ate, I told Claude the Second about the school garden. I promised I would grow fresh carrots, just for him.

Then I took out my math

homework so Mom would see me studying when she walked through the door.

"*Muy bien.*" Mom looked over my paper. "I'm proud of you."

Like he did on most nights, David drove Mom home after work. He helped her make dinner and then stayed to eat.

As we sat down, David asked a question. "What should we get for Mr. Vaslov? His birthday is the Sunday after next. He'll be coming for Sunday dinner, like always."

"I'll make a chocolate cake," Mom said. "But we still need a present."

"He wants a meteorite," I said. "I'm going to find one for him."

"Give it a try, Freddie," David said. "You could get super lucky."

"*¿Es tan difícil?*" Mom asked.

"*Sí,*" David said. "While hundreds land every year, finding one is not easy."

Suddenly, rocks dropping from the sky didn't sound so good. What if one landed on my head?

The next morning, my teacher, Mrs. Blaine, started the day with the big news.

"We're going to grow vegetables in our school garden again!"

Geraldo raised his hand to ask a question. "Will we have to eat them?"

"You'll want to," Mrs. Blaine promised. "Food fresh from the garden tastes amazing."

Claude the Second was going to like that.

"Can we grow carrots?" I asked.

"Definitely." Mrs. Blaine smiled. "I want you to see how some vegetables grow underneath the soil and some grow above."

"Carrots grow underground?" Jason asked.

That question got Mrs. Blaine started on a lesson.

"When you eat spinach," she said, "you're eating the leaf of the plant. A carrot is a root."

All day, Mrs. Blaine was plant crazy. In math, we did word problems, multiplying seeds. In science, we talked about photosynthesis, the way plants make oxygen for the air we breathe. I had no idea there were so many things you could learn about plants.

As we left school, Mrs. Blaine passed out flyers for us to take home.

"Saturday will be Garden Day," she said. "Come with your family."

I waved goodbye to Mrs. Blaine and pressed the buttons on my wristband to turn on my Zapato Power. It was time to find that meteorite for Mr. Vaslov's birthday.

ZOOM! ZOOM! ZAPATO!

Mr. Vaslov had said to look for dark stones with funny shapes. I circled trees and flower gardens.

ZOOM! ZOOM! ZAPATO!

Just like before, I needed more than super speed. I turned on my

super bounce to look at things
from above.

Boing! Boing! Boing!

In the air, I could see things
I'd missed. Like a bumpy-looking
black rock the size of my fist, near
Building A.

Finally! A rock that seemed

special enough to come from
outer space.

ZIP! ZIP! ZaPaTO!

And of course, that's exactly
when Amy came running up.

4. Dr. Digas

"Let's test your rock," Amy said. "I have a magnet."

A magnet was a good idea. I wished I'd thought of it before Amy did.

"It sticks!" Amy shouted. "We should show this rock to Mr. Vaslov!"

ZIP! ZIP! Zapato

Amy was off in a blink. I wondered again, did Mr. Vaslov give Amy extra speed?

ZOOM! ZOOM! Zapato!

As hard as I tried, I couldn't catch up with her before she reached Mr. Vaslov's toolshed.

This was something I needed to talk to Mr. Vaslov about. Except he was busy talking to someone I'd never seen before.

"Hi, Freddie!" Mr. Vaslov

waved. "Meet my friend, Dr. Digas. She's a meteorite specialist."

Dr. Digas was interested in the fireball we saw Sunday night.

"Many people sent in reports," Dr. Digas said. "So there's a chance a fresh meteorite is nearby."

Amy held up the bumpy black rock I'd found. "Could this be one?

It stuck to my magnet."

Dr. Digas examined my rock. "A magnet is only one test. Another test is a streak test. We need an unglazed tile."

"I have one in my toolshed," Mr. Vaslov said.

We went inside to watch Dr. Digas scratch my bumpy black

rock across the tile.

"Do you see that black streak?" Dr. Digas asked. "A freshly fallen meteorite does not leave a mark."

Once again, I saw Mr. Vaslov's face fall. I was disappointed too. What if I couldn't find the meteorite before his birthday?

Dr. Digas stayed a little while longer to answer a few of my questions.

"Does a meteorite give off an outer space beep? Something that could help us track it down?"

I was still hoping my super hearing could help.

"No," Dr. Digas said. "Some people hear a hissing sound when they see a very bright meteor. The sound doesn't last long."

I took a breath before I asked the question most on my mind.

"Could a meteorite hurt someone?"

"It's unlikely," Dr. Digas said. "Most meteorites fall in the ocean or places where people don't live."

"Most" was not "all." I was still worried when Amy and I left Mr. Vaslov's toolshed to go home.

"Have you ever thought about

rocks falling from the sky?" I
asked her.

"And hitting me on the head?"
she asked.

"Yes," I admitted.

"I guess it could happen," Amy
said. "It's not one of the things
moms warn kids about, like running
in the street or talking to strangers."

Amy made me feel better. If outer
space rocks were a real problem,
my mom would want me to wear a
helmet or at least warn me to look
up when I left the house.

The next day at school, Mrs. Blaine had us work together in groups. We scooped dirt into cups and chose seeds. My seeds were tiny. It was hard to believe something that little could grow big enough for my guinea pig to eat.

After the cups were planted, we put them on the windowsill.

"We'll track the progress of our seeds on this graph." Mrs. Blaine held up a big chart.

"I hope mine comes up first," Hamza said.

"It's not a race," Mrs. Blaine said. "Some seeds, like beans, will germinate more quickly."

"What about carrots?" I asked.

"Carrots can be slow," Mrs. Blaine answered. "It will be interesting to compare."

I wasn't happy to hear my carrots could be slow. The next

ing Mrs. Blaine said didn't make me any happier.

"Every spring we study poetry. This year, in honor of our garden, we will write poems about plants."

A poem? I'd never written a poem before!

"And we will read them aloud in class," Mrs. Blaine continued.

¡Ay, no! I had to write a poem and read it to everybody? The thought gave me a headache worse than worrying about a rock falling from the sky.

At recess, Amy rushed across the playground and stopped me before I could get to the basketball court to play with Hamza and Geraldo.

"Freddie!" she called. "There's a problem!"

Starwood Elementary doesn't have a lot of superhero jobs. I was surprised Amy was bringing me one.

"Mrs. Jeffers from the office came by Room 12," Amy said. "She wanted to know if Mr. Newton had seen Mrs. Connor."

"Did he?" I asked.

"No," Amy said, "so Mrs. Jeffers went to Room 13 and Room 14 to ask the same thing."

Amy was right. That sounded strange.

"Could you use your super hearing?" Amy asked. "To find out what's wrong?"

Amy might be faster than I was, but this was a hero job only I could do.

ZOOM! ZOOM! zaPaTO!

I ran to the office and stood behind two tall plants. From there, I could turn on my super hearing without anyone seeing me.

Mrs. Jeffers was on the phone. Her voice was worried.

"Mrs. Connor left her walkie-talkie

on her desk. I can't reach her. It's been an hour."

An hour was a long time to be missing, especially for a principal.

"I've checked every classroom," Mrs. Jeffers said. "Where could she be?"

ZOOM! ZOOM! ZAPATO!

If Mrs. Connor wasn't inside, maybe she was outside.

ZOOM! ZOOM! ZAPATO!

I ran through the playground. No Mrs. Connor. I looked by the back doors and along the brick walls, my ears ready for any sound.

ZOOM! ZOOM! ZAPATO!

Where was Mrs. Connor? Finally, I heard someone moaning on the far side of the school, near the garden.

*"I hope I didn't break anything.
This hurts a lot."*

ZOOM! ZOOM! ZaPaTo!

I found Mrs. Connor sitting on
the ground, rubbing her leg. She
was surprised to see me.

"Freddie?" she asked. "How did
you find me?"

"I have good hearing," I said.

"Was I moaning that loudly?"
She rubbed her leg again.

"It hurts when you trip," I said.
"I fell over one of these garden
beds too."

Freddie!" Mrs. Connor held up
her hand. "I'm not going to ask you
when you were out here or why
you're not with your class now."

"Thank you," I said.

"But please run and get Mrs.
Jeffers for me. I forgot my walkie-
talkie."

A little while later, an
ambulance came. Two paramedics
put Mrs. Connor on a stretcher.

"Will she be okay?" I asked Mrs.
Jeffers.

"Yes." Mrs. Jeffers put a hand on my shoulder. "Thanks to you, Freddie."

This was the kind of hero job I liked the best. When I got to save a grown-up!

But I hadn't done it all by myself.

ZIP! ZIP! ZAPATO

Amy ran up as soon as she saw the ambulance.

"What happened?" she asked.

"Mrs. Connor fell in the garden," I said.

"I'm glad you found her, Freddie."

"I'm glad you told me she was missing." I smiled.

Amy smiled back, just as the two paramedics rolled Mrs. Connor by on the stretcher.

"I'll be back for Garden Day!" Mrs. Connor promised.

"I'll be there too," Amy said. "With my parents."

I was planning to come with Mom and David. Looking around at the tall weeds everywhere, I hoped we'd have a lot of people on Saturday. The school sure needed help before anyone could plant the seeds growing on our classroom

windowsills. No wonder Mrs.
Connor tripped. You could hardly
see the wooden planting boxes
underneath all the grass and leaves.

Thinking about that made me
wonder if something else might
be hidden under a leaf. Like a
meteorite that fell to the ground last
Sunday night.

6. Garden Day

On Saturday, Mrs. Connor was walking on crutches and looking a lot happier.

"Welcome!" she said over and over. "I'm thrilled to see so many families here."

RUFF! RUFF!

Mrs. Connor wasn't quite as glad to see my next-door neighbor

Gio with his little dog, Puppy.

RUFF! RUFF!

Puppy had to go home because he was barking too much. I offered to do the job, and Gio's mom, Mrs. Santos, made me feel like a hero.

"You're the best, Freddie!" She handed me her key. "Be sure to lock Puppy inside the house."

ZOOM! ZOOM! ZAPATO!

When I got back, everywhere I looked, I saw kids and grown-ups working hard. I gave Mrs. Santos her key and joined David in a garden bed. He had a little rake that looked like a claw. With it, he pulled up roots and a small, round rock. Seeing the rock reminded me of something I needed.

ZOOM! ZOOM! ZaPaTO!

I ran over to where Amy was working. "Did you bring your magnet?"

"I don't think magnets pull weeds, Freddie," she said.

"Not for the weeds," I said. "For the rocks."

"Good thought!" She touched her wristband to turn on her super speed. "I'll go get it."

ZIP! ZIP! ZAPATO

Amy was back in a blink, and we worked side by side. With the magnet, we could test any black rocks that turned up.

Each raised garden box needed its tall weeds cleared out. Amy and I had to stand up to grab the green tops. Most of the roots didn't want to come out, so it was like playing tug-of-war.

"The weeds are winning!" Amy said.

I took a turn pulling on a big one that was giving Amy trouble.

The weed was too strong for me too.

UGH! I fell over. Amy giggled. Soon we were both laughing and falling backward, trying to pull out weeds as high as our waists.

Mr. Escobar, Amy's dad, came over with a big clipper and snipped the thick stems closer to the ground.

"Now you need a hand tool," Mr. Escobar said, "to loosen the roots."

I remembered David's little rake and looked for him. He was on the other side of the garden, pushing a wheelbarrow.

ZOOM! ZOOM! ZaPaTO!

One of the best things about my super zapatos is the Zapato

Power smoke. When I run, I'm
covered in a cloud of invisible
smoke. Sometimes people notice
when I disappear, but the people
who know me have gotten used
to it. They just think I'm fast.
¡Muy rápido!

ZOOM! ZOOM! ZAPATO!

I caught up with David as he
was dumping dirt into one of the
garden beds.

"Could I use your little rake?" I
asked.

"I gave it to your mom,"

David said. "She's with Mrs. Santos, setting up water for the volunteers."

ZOOM⚡ZOOM⚡ZAPATO⚡

I found my mom at the refreshment table.

"*Sí*," Mom said. "It's here."

She handed me a bag with gardening gloves and the little rake. Two things I could use.

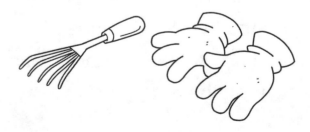

ZOOM! ZOOM! ZAPATO!

Back at the garden bed, Amy
and I had luck with the little rake.
The claw really loosened things
up. Woody roots came out of the
ground, along with balls of dirt.
And something else. ROCKS!

Amy was in charge of testing
them with her magnet. The first
ones we found did not stick, but
then we came across a shiny black
rock sitting beside a weed. This
rock had an odd shape, and it was
heavy in my hand.

"The magnet is sticking!" Amy said.

Could it be true? Did we find a meteorite?

David came over with his wheelbarrow. He dumped the dirt, and we helped him spread it.

"We're finished," David said. "This was the last bed."

I looked around. The garden

wasn't a mess anymore. Every raised wooden box was filled with fresh, dark soil, ready for planting. Lots of people had come together to make something special happen.

And Amy and I had worked together to find a black rock that might be a meteorite.

7. Dreaming

We showed the shiny black rock to Mr. Vaslov. Right away, he liked it.

"It feels heavy," he said. "Good sign!"

We did the streak test. No black mark on the tile!

Then Mr. Vaslov picked up a file and scraped off a tiny part of the rock so we could see inside.

"Look!" He pointed. "Metal spots."

"Is that a good sign too?" Amy asked.

"Yes!" Mr. Vaslov grinned. "I'm going to ask Dr. Digas where I should send this for testing."

"What will you do if the rock is a real meteorite?" Amy asked.

"I'll study it," Mr. Vaslov said. "A rock from outer space could have special properties no one knows about yet. It could help me with my inventions."

"Could you make inventions with even more superpowers?" I asked.

Mr. Vaslov winked. "You never know."

"I'd like to be able to fly," Amy said.

"Freddie and I have talked about a rocket backpack," Mr. Vaslov said. "Any other ideas?"

"What about a special hat that helps you understand any language?" Amy asked.

We spent the rest of the afternoon dreaming up inventions. As we talked, Amy made sketches on pieces of paper.

"You're quite an artist," Mr. Vaslov said. "Do you draw at school?"

"I do," Amy answered. "Mr. Newton says pictures help us write good stories."

Talking about school reminded me of the poem I had to write for Mrs. Blaine's class.

"I have writing homework this weekend," I said. "It won't be easy."

"Let me draw you a picture," Amy said. "It will help."

Amy drew a plant pushing out

of the ground for me to
take home. After staring
at it for a while, I came up
with some words I liked for my poem.
I just wished I didn't have to read it
aloud in class.

On Monday morning, Mrs. Blaine
called us up in alphabetical order to
read our poems. Hamza had to go
first because his last name starts with
an "A."

"Glad to have that over with," he
said as he sat down.

My last name starts with "R," so I had lots of time to think about standing in front of everybody and hearing my voice come out as a squeak.

When I get nervous, I fiddle with my Zapato Power wristband. That turns on my super hearing. And that means I can hear what's happening outside in the hallway.

"Oh no! What am I going to do about this?"

I recognized Mrs. Connor's voice. She had another problem. Could I take a bathroom pass and slip out? We were only up to

Jasmin, whose last name started with a "C."

ZOOM! ZOOM! ZAPATO!

At the end of the hall, I saw Mrs. Connor on her crutches. She was staring sadly at a bunch of pencils scattered over the floor.

"What happened, Mrs. Connor?" I asked.

"Freddie!" She looked up. "What are you doing here?"

For once, I didn't have to worry about being in trouble, because I

had a bathroom pass. But that wasn't
the real reason I was in the hallway.

"You need help," I said.

Mrs. Connor sighed. "I do. I
spilled these pencils."

"It's not easy to walk on crutches
and carry things," I said.

This was something I knew
firsthand from when I broke my
ankle.

Mrs. Connor sighed again. "I'm trying to do too much with an injured leg."

"Let me pick up the pencils," I said.

Mrs. Connor leaned on her crutches and watched. "Maybe it's not so bad that you're always in the hallway, Freddie."

The chance to do a hero job took my mind off having to read out loud. I wasn't scared anymore when I walked back into class.

"It's your turn to share, Freddie," Mrs. Blaine said.

I picked up my paper and

cleared my throat. Every word
came out fine.

> If a seed as small as a freckle
> can grow up strong and tall,
> then I can believe my dream
> will come true after all.

In my poem, I wasn't just
thinking about a carrot seed. I was
thinking about the black shiny
rock and how I hoped it was a
meteorite. Were we going to know
in time for Mr. Vaslov's birthday?

8. Mr. Vaslov's Birthday

Amy and I checked in with Mr. Vaslov every day after school.

"Did you hear from the lab?"

And every day, we got the same answer.

"Not yet."

"Why is it taking so long?" Amy asked on Friday.

"A meteorite has to be carefully

analyzed," Mr. Vaslov said.

"I don't like waiting," Amy complained.

"No one does." Mr. Vaslov pointed to the side of his toolshed where we'd piled up rocks that were not meteorites. "I've been waiting for someone to help me spread these stones back out over Starwood Park."

"I'll do it!" Amy said.

ZIP! ZIP! ZAPATO!

Amy gathered an armful and headed off. For once, I liked seeing her go first. I finally had a chance to talk to Mr. Vaslov alone.

"Amy is really fast," I began.

Mr. Vaslov nodded. "You noticed."

"Did you make her shoes faster than mine?"

"A little," he said. "After all, you have super hearing and super bounce."

Looking at it that way, it didn't seem too unfair.

"In a team," Mr. Vaslov said, "people help each other by doing what each does best."

"So Amy will be the fastest one on our team?" I asked.

Mr. Vaslov nodded.

I could live with that. Amy always did her part. And she'd given me a chance to do mine when she told me Mrs. Connor was missing.

ZIP! ZIP! ZaPaTO

Amy came back for another armful of rocks. I joined her.

ZOOM! ZOOM! ZaPaTO!

As soon as we were finished, Amy asked about the lab results again.

"When will we know?"

"I hope by Sunday," I said. "That's Mr. Vaslov's birthday."

"Is there going to be a party?" Amy asked.

"At my house," I said. "Do you want to come?"

"Yes!" Amy said. "I'll go home and start on my present."

ZIP! ZIP! ZAPATO

What was Amy going to make for Mr. Vaslov? And what could I give him? Mom and David had bought him a red sweater that they said was from all of us. But a meteorite would be a whole lot better.

On Sunday afternoon, Amy came to my house with a packet of pictures she had drawn. The best one showed me flying with a rocket backpack.

"Very cool!" I said.

"Mr. Vaslov likes to dream,"

Amy said. "So I drew the things we dreamed about."

While Mom frosted the cake and David finished dinner, Amy helped me with decorations. We blew up balloons and hung a Happy Birthday banner. At six o'clock, when Mr. Vaslov knocked on the door, we were ready.

"Happy Birthday!" we shouted.

"WOW! Thank you!"

Mr. Vaslov came inside, carrying a box.

"Why do you have a present for us?" Amy asked. "It's your birthday."

Mr. Vaslov shook his head. "This came from the meteorite lab."

"What did they say?" I asked.

"I don't know," he answered. "I've been too nervous to see what's inside."

David took a deep breath. "The moment of truth."

"I have my fingers crossed," Mom said.

"Mine are too," I said.

"So who's going to open the box?" Amy asked.

Mr. Vaslov held the box out to me. "Go ahead, Freddie."

I ripped it open before anyone could blink.

"Show us!" Amy shouted.
Inside, I found our black rock and a

letter, which I gave to Mr. Vaslov.

He read it silently.

"Did we find a meteorite?" Amy jumped up and down.

Mr. Vaslov grinned. "Yes! The black rock we sent in for testing has been identified as a meteorite from outer space."

YAY! We cheered! We hugged! We danced around!

For the rest of the night, Mr. Vaslov's smile was as bright as a meteor in the sky.

Don't Miss Freddie's Other Adventures!

HC 978-0-8075-9480-3
PB 978-0-8075-9479-7

PB 978-0-8075-9483-4

PB 978-0-8075-9484-1

HC 978-0-8075-9485-8
PB 978-0-8075-9486-5

HC 978-0-8075-9487-2
PB 978-0-8075-9496-4

HC 978-0-8075-9497-1
PB 978-0-8075-9499-5

HC 978-0-8075-9500-8
PB 978-0-8075-9542-8

HC 978-0-8075-9539-8
PB 978-0-8075-9559-6

HC 978-0-8075-9544-2
PB 978-0-8075-9563-3

HC 978-0-8075-9562-6
PB 978-0-8075-9567-1